Duty to the Heart

Polemos

J.R. Baler

For all the believers,
remember that love is out there
if you truly follow what's in
your heart. ~ J.R. Baler

Prologue

The End of a Chapter

"Your highness, your father wants to see you."

Looking up from his studies in his chambers, twenty-two-year-old Prince Louis kept his voice calm and a stoic look on his face. "Where is he?" was all he asked.

"In his chambers," responded the experienced member of the royal staff.

Standing up from behind his desk, Louis looked the man straight in the eyes. Everything he needed to know appeared in the man's eyes. "Take me to him."

The pair made their way through the palace on the late Autumn evening. Trees banged against the glass, as the wind whistled and echoed through the near empty corridors. Louis did his best to ignore the stormy weather that was rapidly approaching outside, as he made his way down the corridor with the sole companion until the pair reached a set of closed wooden doors. Stepping forward, the elder gentleman knocked on the door and then stepped to the side for the young prince, who hurriedly entered the room.

It was hard to maintain his breathing by this point, as the heir to the throne kneeled by his father's bedside, ignoring protocol in which he would have normally been formally introduced. He then took the king's hand and softly spoke, "Father?"

"Louis?" King Phillip weakly uttered, as his hand enclosed over his son's hand. "It is time."

Every emotion flooded through Louis' mind, as he tried to keep his composure and let everything come flying out of his mouth. It was only with one small breath and a tear near coming out of his eye did he feel something. He looked up to see Queen Elizabeth's hand on his shoulder, as she stood next to him. This small act of compassion reminded the prince that he would not be alone, though it would not lessen the heartache of what he was about to endure. "… Yes, Father…"

"Do as I have taught you… and trust your heart…" softly spoke the king, as he moved his free hand over his son's heart.

Catching his breath in his throat, as his chest grew tight, the young prince was failing at controlling his emotions. A single tear then found its way down his cheek. "I will…"

The old ruler then leaned back and turned his head towards the opened window, as leaves started to fly by. "I wish I could have seen her again…."

With those last words, the room fell dark, as the candles were blown out.

∞ ∞ ∞

Chapter One
Valiaguila

In the busy port in the kingdom of Valiaguila, Izzy wandered around the market with a basketful of food to take back to the ship. She no longer resembled the princess that she used to be with her regal dresses. As a sailor, she adjusted to pants and boots to maneuver around the ship, although that did not stop her from buying a few simple dresses for when she was in port.

She had rarely been to Valiaguila, in fact, this was only her second time as Drake tried to avoid the kingdom. Ever since he gave up captaining the Tesoro, he had wanted to distance himself from the world he had grown up in, which included his childhood home. Since Izzy was alone at the moment, she wanted to take the opportunity to try to see what it was like, and everything seemed quite different from Dauphin Magie. Instead of the white and blue color palettes of the buildings, there was red and gold with a slightly more angular edging compared to the roundness of her buildings. The kingdom was wealthy beyond measure, probably thanks to privateers like Black Spot Jack and Drake the Dread. Of course, even with their vast wealth, there were the common folk, who sold the everyday uses in the market by the port. Everything was very hustle and bustle, and not quite as serene as Dauphin Magie.

However, as chaotic and different from her former home as it was, Izzy still wanted to see more. Eventually, she did come to a stop by a flower stand and took in the beautiful fragrance of the orchids, her favorite flower. Just the smell brought back all of her childhood memories from when she would venture outside of the palace and bring them back home. Her mother had always kept roses around the palace, but the young girl always snuck in all of the colors of the rainbow with the orchids and placed them around her room.

"Happy Anniversary, Izzy."

The young girl turned to see her husband, standing behind her with a bouquet of red, pink, purple, and white orchids in his right hand, which sported a black leather glove. He wore a smile on his face, as he held the florae out to her. "Oh, Drake! They're beautiful! Thank you!" the former royal spoke, as she leaned over to embrace him.

"I can't believe it's been three years," he spoke in amazement.

"Three wonderful years," the former royal responded.

"And may there be many more in our future," and he kissed her brow.

A smile came to Izzy's face before she looked up into the sailor's eyes. She knew it was now or never if she wanted to see where her husband had grown up. "Drake, I know that you don't like to visit here very often, but since we are here… could you please show me around?"

Drake looked back into her eyes, and he could see that this was a topic that she would not give up. He then took a deep breath and realized it was time to surrender. "I guess we could do a small tour of some of the old areas that I used to live in."

"Thank you, Drake. You have no idea how much this means to me by you going back into that part of your life."

The young man reached out, took the basket from his wife, and then offered his arm before escorting her further back into the kingdom. He had to take a deep breath with those first few steps, as he had not ventured past the port in many years, and memories were starting to flood back to him. To try to keep his mind focused, all he could do was point out the various places to Izzy and try to keep any childhood recollections from taking over his emotions. “So, up on top of the hillside is the palace, to keep an eye over the entire kingdom.”

“Similar to how my castle was placed,” replied Izzy.

Drake just let out a little laughter. “I guess all royals need to make sure to keep a constant eye on their subjects.”

“And see what more could be done to help them,” added in Izzy with a knowing smile.

“Aye, your majesty,” and Drake continued on. “These streets moving north started to separate the classes. The more money you had, the closer to the palace you were. In fact, if you look at all of the designs, you will see which ones become more ornate if you go in that direction.”

“Everything is so pretty here…”

A genuine smile of fondness came to the boy’s lips. “Yeah… it is a really pretty kingdom,” and then all of a sudden, he stopped cold and stared at a house that remained in shambles.

“Drake, what’s wrong?”

All he could do was stare at the charred structure, as memories flooded back and took over. “I can’t believe I brought us here.”

“Is this where you lived?” Izzy asked with concern, and Drake nodded his head. “I’m so sorry. We don’t have to stay.”

“No… No, Izzy. I think I need to face this,” and he stepped through the hole in the wall before Izzy and placed the basket down on what was left of a table. Nothing had changed since that night when he was six years old, aside from a few things that were taken. He then stepped further in and found the blood-stained curtain on the floor. As he fell to his knees next to the worn fabric, all he could see were the ghosts reliving that terrible night.

"Mama!" he cried, as he fell to his knees next to his pale mother.

"Drake..." she whispered. "... I'm so glad you're fine."

"Mama..." Drake started to cry, as he put his hands on his mother. A gasp then escaped his mouth and his eyes grew wide, as he pulled his hands back to find blood on them. "What's going on?"

"I'm so... so sorry... Drake..." she tried to say with tears in her eyes.

"Anne!" cried out a sea captain, as he ran into the room and fell to his knees beside the young boy and his mother. "What happened?"

"They... They came... for you... Jack..." softly spoke Anne.

"Drake... kiss your mother goodbye and go and gather all of your belongings. You're coming back with me to the Tesoro," said Captain Black Spot Jack.

Hearing the seriousness in his father's tone, all Drake could do was nod, lean over his mother, and with his free arm, wrap it around her. He never let go of her hand, as he gave her a kiss and whispered, "I love you, Mama..."

"I love you too... Drake..." Anne replied back with a barely audible voice.

A hand then gently touched Drake's shoulder, as he remembered his mother saying his name, and he jumped back to see his wife standing over him. "Are you alright?"

Breathing hard, the lad looked around the room. Everything had seemed so real, like it had happened all over again right in front of his eyes. However, after a few moments to let his heart calm down, Drake reminded himself that it was just a vivid memory back to haunt him. He closed his eyes and then ran his gloved hand through his hair, just as a physical reminder that he was indeed physically in his house at this very time and not sixteen years ago. After opening his eyes, he then looked down into the rawhide material that covered his hand and then formed it into a fist. "Aye… Aye, I'm fine, Izzy."

"I'm so sorry, Drake," and she kneeled down to pull him into a hug.

The young man sat frozen for a moment before he slowly put his arms around her and clutched at the back of her dress like a scared little boy. All he could do was remain silent in grief for several minutes and shed a tear or two. It did not matter that he was now twenty- two years old, he still had that emotional six-year-old boy inside of him. A little boy who loved his mother and missed her terribly.

"It is alright to cry if you need to. I'm here," softly spoke Izzy, trying to console him.

For a few minutes more, Drake started sobbing and let the tears fall until there was no more to be found. He had let the emotions get the best of him, but for the moment, it was what he needed. Since that night, he had not had a good cry like that and it had all caught up to him. When the boy found he could cry no more, he took a deep breath to let his mind clear and then leaned back to look at the girl holding him with a small smile. "Thank you, Izzy. It was just what I needed."

"Would you like to leave?" she asked with a smile, wanting to make sure he took all the time he needed.

With a nod of his head, the captain stood up and offered his hand to help Izzy up. He then quietly turned to walk out, but took one last look back at the place he hoped he would never again see. Picking up the small basket, he then emerged out onto the streets where his wife was already waiting on him.

"So, where to next, Captain?" asked the young lady, as she held on to her bouquet and brought it closer to her.

Drake smiled down upon the young lady before turning her in the direction of the ship, as he took her arm. He quickly tried to put on a cheery disposition thinking of the surprise he had in store. "Well, I heard the little island of Papillon de Baleine had a plethora of silk to trade for cheap."

Izzy's eyes widened with excitement. "That's near the main island of Dauphin Magie!"

A smile came to the sailor's lips, as he nodded. "I thought we might be able to take a slight detour to say 'hi', after we did some trading."

"Drake, that would be wonderful!" exclaimed Izzy, and she leaned up to kiss his cheek.

"Anything for you," he replied with a smile, now back to his old self and remembering that today was supposed to be a happy day. "And wait until you see what I have in store for you tonight."

"And what's that?"

"Well, I would tell you, but I don't want to spoil the surprise," he replied with a wink and kissed her.

"Ah, young love," a raspy voice spoke, and the couple looked over to see an elderly lady, resting her weight on a knotted, wooden cane. Her silver hair flowed out from under her scarf that was draped over her head. "Celebrating something special?"

"Why yes," began Izzy, as Drake moved his arm from holding her arm to around her shoulders. "It's our anniversary."

"That is something special indeed," replied the woman, as she reached into her cloak, and Drake pulled his wife back into him to protect her. The woman then pulled out a crystal rose. "Congratulations!" and she handed it to Izzy.

"It's so beautiful. Thank-" and as the former princess touched the crystal, it turned blood red.

"You!" started the lady, her voice growing deeper and her eyes gleaming a vibrant violet. "There is a strong vision I see of your future."

"Izzy, let's go," and Drake tried to lead her away.

"No, Drake. My father always taught me to listen and heed all warnings," replied Izzy, and she turned her attention back to the bewitching lady. "What is it?"

"Blood red stones sit upon your brow, but will fall when showers of ash and fire over take your world," and Izzy retracted into the arms of her husband, as the red rose turned black. "However, streaks of purple and blue will bring you hope when you need it most," and the black rose became transparent again.

"Enough!" commanded Drake, keeping his wife safe. "We've heard enough," he spoke in a calmer voice. "Let's go, Izzy," and he led her away.

"You have been warned!" called the elderly woman, and when Izzy looked back over her shoulder, the woman was gone.

"Drake, what do you think she meant by that?" asked the young woman, as they entered the busy market place.

"I'm not sure," started the sailor, and then he tried to think about what he could say to put her mind at ease. "Whatever it is, it can't be too bad. She did say there was hope in your future," and he winked at her. In truth, the warning even had him a little on edge.

"I hope you're right, Drake," sighed Izzy, as they began to exit the crowd and step on to the docks.

"No matter what, we're in this together," he smiled and escorted his wife on to the ship. Within the hour, they were sailing for Papillon de Baleine and more importantly Izzy's home in Dauphin Magie.

Chapter Two

Papillon de Baleine

Izzy and Drake stood just outside of the ballroom on the balcony, holding each other's hand. The princess then looked up at her friend, her heart breaking. "... Louis told you everything, didn't he?"

All Drake could do was nod his head, as he pulled her hand closer to him. "I don't think I could do this without you. You taught me to trust my heart and that I could be a better person for it. And if I'm to lead this life among royalty, I want you there with me. If not... I need to go back to the sea to be myself."

"If only we could have more time together," whispered Izzy, as a tear came to her eye.

Drake moved his hand to dry her cheek before resting his hand on that spot. "Shh... this isn't goodbye. We will meet again," and he leaned in to kiss her.

They held onto that moment for what seemed like a lifetime, neither one of them wanting it to end. It was only the sound of a man clearing his throat, which brought them back to reality. Slowly, they pulled apart to see King Philip had joined them outside, away from the rest of the guests. A look of sheer embarrassment over took the two young people's faces, at the sight of the elder ruler intruding. "Bella... Drake..." he said in a low, collected voice.

"I am so sorry. Please excuse me, your majesty," spoke Drake with a slight bow, and he gently let go of Izzy's hand before slowly stepping away and heading towards his room for the remainder of the evening.

"Daddy, please let me explain..." started Izzy, stepping towards her father.

"Bella... what kind of behavior is this? You know what your duties are as princess, and it is not fair to lead this young man on when you know what you must do."

"But, Daddy... I love him," she uttered quietly, as if admitting it for the first time to not only the world but herself.

King Philip gradually walked over towards his daughter and pulled her into his arms to hold her close to him. This caught the seventeen-year-old girl completely off guard, as she was prepared to hear a lecture about how she could not love someone, whom she had just re-met after only spending a few months with as children or how she should not have feelings for someone whom was not her betrothal. None-the-less, she stayed in her father's arms and buried her head in his chest, trying to hold back tears. "Bella..." he started. "As your king, I cannot allow such behavior, but as your father... I can see the truth in your eyes. I haven't seen you this happy since your eleventh birthday when you danced with Drake at your ball. As your father, I want nothing more than your happiness and to know that you will be with someone that you love and will love you back. Both men, Prince Adonis and Sir Drake, are honorably and would do anything for you. So... It sounds like you have a choice to make. Duty to your kingdom or duty to your heart. You know whatever your heart chooses, I will always be proud of you and love you."

"You're leaving this decision up to me?" Izzy spoke, as she lifted her head back to look into her father's eyes.

"Yes..." responded Philip with a smile. "I want you to be happy. You are first and foremost, my daughter. Your happiness means the world to me."

With tears in her eyes, Izzy leaned up to kiss Philip on the cheek. "I love you, Daddy. Thank you."

"I love you too, my Bella," replied King Philip with a tender smile on his face.

∞ ∞ ∞

"Daddy..." uttered Izzy, as her eyelids flashed open. Staying mostly still, her eyes scanned the area to see that she was in a cabin on a ship. It took her a few minutes to realize she was not the seventeen-year-old girl anymore, but a twenty-year-old married woman living on a small ship with her husband as merchant traders.

"Good morning, Izzy," greeted Drake, as he walked into the room. He then took note of the confused look on her face and sat down on the bed beside her. "Are you alright?"

"I had a dream... and it felt so real," she started, as she finally sat up and moved her hand to her head. "It was the last time I saw my father.... I just miss him, my mother, and Louis so much."

Drake put his arms around Izzy and pulled her into a comforting hug, as she started to cry. "Shh... it's alright. You will get to see them soon."

Hearing her husband's words and feeling his hand softly stroke her hair comforted the young girl, stopping the tears from becoming sobs. He was right, soon she would be able to go home and see her family that she had not seen in over three years. Of course, the only way to do that is to sneak into the palace, undetected. While out sailing, she had overheard people talk about how the Princess of Dauphin Magie was lost at sea, something she figured her father had told the Court to get her out of her betrothal. She knew that her visit was going to have to be as secretive as possible. "Thank you, Drake. What would I ever do without you?" she asked with a grateful smile.

"You would be perfectly fine. You can take care of yourself and others," he replied, as he kissed the top of her head.

"But I am a much better person with you by my side."

"As am I," and he looked up as the sun light started to fill the room. "So, what do you say to exploring Papillon de Baleine?"

"I think an adventure is exactly what I need," and she slid out of bed, ready for what the small island would bring.

∞ ∞ ∞

As the couple descended down the gang plank to walk on shore of Papillon de Baleine, they noticed an eerie stillness in the air. It was a very small island, but it usually had a gay feeling about, as smiles were always on the faces of the people and bright, colorful fabric was used for tapestries and clothing. This day was the exact opposite that Izzy had known this area to be. There was a dark shroud that covered the area and sent a chill up the two sailors' spines, as they walked deeper into the villages.

Drake even took note on how the streets were near empty and kept an eye out for the smallest detail that could give him any clue as to what was going on. The one person he spotted, who was covered in black, let her head hang low and an opaque veil cover her face. She carried black roses in her hand, as she sluggishly made her way down the roads. "Someone has passed on…" uttered the former pirate.

"Do you think a family member?" asked Izzy.

Shaking his head, Drake kept an eye on the elder woman. "I think it was someone of great importance for everyone to be in mourning," as he started to take note of the black fabric that covered all of the windows of the homes.

"We should keep walking. Maybe we'll find out more information of what is happening," spoke up Izzy, starting to move forward. "Plus, we need to find that great deal on silk, because that is why we came here," she added with a small wink.

A small knowing grin came to Drake's face as he heard the last comment. "Well… maybe one of the reasons," and they both shared in a laugh as they moved deeper into town. "Besides, if I see your brother, I need to challenge him to a fencing duel. We'll see if he got better with practice," and Drake pulled out his sword and swung it around a few times.

Izzy could not help but laugh. "You just want to show off your fancy fencing glove."

"Maybe," Drake shrugged with a small grin, before he sheathed his sword.

"I know it means a lot to you, Drake, but are you ever going to take it off?"

"Never," replied the sailor with a big grin, before he escorted his wife further into the community.

More and more people started to fill the streets, the closer the couple got to the hub, holding on to small lit candles and all of their faces were covered. It was a ritual that Izzy had never seen before, and she was familiar with most all traditions within her kingdoms' realms. "Drake, have you ever seen anything like this before?"

"We did something similar back in Valiaguila, when my mother passed away," started Drake, keeping his voice steady as the memories flooded back.

"Was it because your father was important in your kingdom?"

Drake just shook his head a bit, "I honestly don't remember. I was so young that, that part of what happened was a blur. Then when my father passed away, I wasn't on land long enough to see anything. I just wanted to stay out at sea on the Tesoro."

Izzy let her head hang down, as she stopped in her steps. Guilt was filling up her emotions over what she had just said. "I'm sorry, Drake. I know I keep bringing up your mother's death, and I don't mean to. It's just…"

"It's alright, Izzy," started Drake, as he took her hand. "As much as it hurts bringing her up, I'm also glad I can still talk about my mother. It means I haven't forgotten her."

"If you ever need to talk…"

"I know, Izzy. You'll be there to listen," he responded with a smile.

All she could do was smile back before noting that the crowds had formed and stopped in the square. She squeezed Drake's hand for a moment before cautiously making her way to the front of the crowd and looked up to see a thin veil was covering something. Moving forward, she tried to focus on what image was underneath that fabric.

It was only when she was about a foot away that she could piece the shapes together and let out a gasp. "No…"

"What's going on?" spoke up Drake, as he finally made it to his wife's side. Izzy then turned around and started crying into his shoulder, as he put his arms around her. "Shh… it's alright. Everything is going to be alright," but the consoling words did not penetrate the sobs that could not be suppressed. He then looked around and stepped a little bit closer to a teary-eyed lady next to them. "Excuse me," he began and the lady looked up at him from behind her veil. "I am terribly sorry to ask this, but who passed on?"

"You do not know?" she questioned in confusion, and Drake shook his head. "The good King Philip left us twenty-five weeks ago, and his son, Prince Louis, is to be crowned king on the day after tomorrow."

Shock was all the sailor could feel, as he let the words sink into his mind to comprehend and not even notice the lady turning her attention back to the covered portrait. Why had they not heard of this sooner? News like this surely should have made it to the other kingdoms. However, other kingdoms like Valiaguila would not be talking of such a thing, as the two kingdoms did not always see eye to eye. It took Drake a moment, as all of this flooded his mind, before he gently started to escort his wife out of the crowd, so as not to draw any additional attention to them. It was the last thing they needed being so close to her home.

∞ ∞ ∞

"Come here," Drake spoke gently, as he slid into a corner between two buildings and let Izzy just cry into him. "I am so sorry, Izzy. If I had known, I would never have suggested us coming here."

The young girl wanted to say a thousand things. "It's alright. You didn't know," or "This can't be happening", but she just kept sobbing into her husband's shirt. Quietness was the only form of support that he could give her, and it was the only support she wanted to hear for the time being.

When the sobbing started to taper off, Drake finally worked up the courage to speak. "Izzy, I'm so sorry about your father's passing. He was a great man, and he was obviously very loved by everyone he touched. If I could bring him back to you, I would in an instant."

"Thank you, Drake," she whispered, trying to dry her tears with her hands.

Drake helped to dry her tears before speaking. "I know I told you that we would go to the main island of Dauphin Magie, but if you don't want to, we don't have to."

"No… No. I want to go," she started. "I need to see my mother and brother. I have to go home."

Chapter Three

Home Again

"Do you remember how to get in?" asked Drake, standing behind Izzy, as she had her hands tracing along the rocks that made the castle walls. As dawn was rapidly approaching, she had very little light to work with to find the old secret entrance.

The girl stopped and turned around to give her husband a stern look. "I used this entrance almost every day for fourteen years. I think I would remember where it was," and she turned back, as Drake kept an amused grin on his face. She then brushed her hands against some vines to move them to the side. With that one swoop, she turned her head around to face the former buccaneer and gave him a smirk. "See? I told you I remembered," and she made her way inside.

Letting a little laugh escape his mouth, Drake just shook his head. "Same old Izzy, and I wouldn't have it any other way," and he followed her into the secret passage.

∞ ∞ ∞

Carefully the couple made their way down the dark, damp tunnel that led into the palace. No one had used it in over three years, and so the air was mustier than usual, which was quite the opposite of the clean sea breeze that they had become used to. However, even the choking on the stale atmosphere that brought about a fit in their lungs did not deter them from their purpose. Quietness consumed the tunnels, except for the faint drip of water that fell from the ceiling to the dirt grounds.

It was only after they had made it about halfway down the tunnel that Drake had to ask a question that had boggled his mind since hearing the passing of the King Philip. "Izzy, why did your kingdom wait so long to have the coronation for your brother? They always knew that he was next in line."

Izzy tried to take a deep breath, which was difficult with the lack of fresh air, before starting her response. "When the first king of Dauphin Magie passed away upon the throne, he left no heir, and the young queen he left behind was so frail, she was about to follow him. So, the kingdom had to search far and wide for someone, who was fit to wear the crown. It took five weeks before they found the new king, who was worthy of the crown. The queen herself gave her blessing to this very young ruler on her deathbed. As the new king was being ready to be crowned, he discovered that the former ruler had only been in power for five years. He then decreed that a period of mourning reflect a ruler's reign, as it had worked out that it had taken five weeks that the kingdom had no official king. Ever since then, the tradition has been honored. Seeing as the period of mourning had lasted twenty-five weeks, my father ruled Dauphin Magie for twenty-five years. I never knew exactly how long, but I knew it had not been much longer than Louis had been alive. Mom and Dad always told me that they were married shortly after he was crowned and not too long after that, Louis was born."

"I guess coincidence helps to make traditions," smiled Drake, as he stayed closely behind Izzy.

"I guess so," laughed Izzy, as the joke made complete sense but at the same time did not. Her laughing did not last long, as she choked on the decayed air.

Drake quickly came up behind his wife, put one hand on her shoulder, and with his other gently hit her back to try to open up her airways a bit. "Easy there," he softly spoke, and when she was finally able to catch her breath, he stopped. "Are you alright?"

"Yes… Yes, I'm fine," she replied, a little woozy. "I probably shouldn't cut off any oxygen to my head down here," Izzy joked, and Drake just smiled and tried to keep from laughing himself.

"No, you shouldn't," he responded with the same lightheartedness.

"We should be nearing the end," the young girl spoke with hope in her voice, if anything to see light and breathe fresh air again. She then slowly put out her hand and felt the large boulder wall in front of her. It took a few moments of relying on her old senses before she recognized the right stone to move that caused the rock to pull back and slide to the side. "I knew I could find it," she said with a smile.

"I never doubted you for a moment," Drake spoke, as he followed her into the open hall.

It was just as Drake had seen the hall the very first time that he had stepped foot into it when he was twelve years old. The sun had just appeared in the sky, and its light hit the diamond chandeliers that adorned the hallways, making the beams dance all around the room. He then looked over to see Izzy standing in the middle of the empty hall, quietly and soaking up all of the memories that she had as a child. Drake remembered her telling him how it was one of her favorite places to be in, but only when it was at this time of the day, and he could only imagine how happy she must feel being back in this spot.

All of the happiness he had for his wife vanished, as he heard a door slowly creak open. “Izzy! Someone’s coming,” he called out in a hushed voice. When he saw no reaction from her, Drake rushed over, grabbed the girl by the shoulders and pulled her behind a giant potted plant. They stayed crouched down and out of sight, but they could not help over hearing the two members of the castle staff talking.

“I cannot believe the coronation is tomorrow,” spoke the younger of the two ladies.

“Well, that explains why the prince is up so early.”

“Our future king has a lot he has to do before he is officially crowned.”

“Which is why he’s having breakfast in his throne room with her majesty, the queen.”

“If you could call this a royal breakfast. It’s just tea and crumpets. Prince Louis always has much more than this and something with chocolate.”

“That is why I put a piece on his tray,” and the two women giggled, as they exited the hallway.”

“Well, at least we know where he is,” smiled Drake.

“I can’t wait to see him and Mother!” exclaimed Izzy, as she jumped out from behind the planter and started to race for the door with Drake emerging behind her. She then collided with a person and fell backwards to the ground.

“Bella?”

Shaking her head, Izzy then looked up at the owner of the voice. “Sir Arthur?”

A smile overtook the old man's worn face, as he reached out a hand to help the young girl up and pulled her into a hug. "It is so good to see you again."

"I'm so happy to see you too," responded the former princess, as she hugged her old advisor back. It was the best feeling to be able to see someone from her childhood once again. Izzy had forgotten how much she had missed her old life and how much she truly missed everyone that was apart of it.

Arthur then looked over to see Drake coming up beside them, and his genuine happy appearance turned into one of duty, as he gave a slight bow of his head. "Sir Drake."

Drake could feel the coldness coming off of the royal advisor, as he accepted the acknowledgement. He knew the older man blamed him for the death of his daughter and the princess of Dauphin Magie abdicating her royal duties. There was nothing he could do or say to comfort Arthur nor would any apology be worthy of the loss that he had suffered. All he knew was he had to watch his wording carefully. "Hello," was all he could muster in the end, as he returned the bow.

The royal advisor then turned his attention back to the former royal with a smile. "I expect that you are here to see your brother and mother," and Izzy nodded her head with a smile. "Let me take you to them. It has been a rather busy morning," and he escorted the couple to the throne room.

∞ ∞ ∞

"Excuse me, your highnesses," spoke Arthur, as he entered the room, and Louis and Elizabeth both looked up from their breakfast and documents surrounding them. "There is someone here to see you."

"Who?" asked Louis, not ready to receive any callers.

"Me," spoke a familiar voice, and both of the royals stood up at the sound. It was then that Izzy stepped into the room with Drake following in behind her.

"Bella…" uttered Elizabeth, as she ran to her daughter and pulled her into her arms. "I never thought I would see you again."

"I didn't think I would ever see you again, Mother," quietly spoke Izzy, and she stayed in her mother's arms, as Louis walked over to the two women in his life.

"Come here, Bella," and the young girl looked up and ran into her brother's open arms. She felt more like herself, as she was with her family.

Arthur just smiled at the scene before he quietly ushered everyone that was not related to the royal family out of the room. Then as he was about to leave, he heard his name and looked back to see Izzy standing before him. She kept her smile on her face before she gave him one last hug and whispered in his ear, "Mary says that she loves you and asks that you forgive everyone involved in her death, even yourself." It was then that a tear came to the old man's eye, and he looked down at the girl who became a woman before his eyes. No words could come to his mouth, so he quietly slipped out of the room and closed the door behind him.

"Drake, it is good to see you again," spoke Elizabeth, as she gave her son-in-law a hug, who was a little surprised at the gesture but very grateful at the same time.

"It's… good to see you too," replied Drake, awkwardly.

Louis then made his way over to the sailor. "Welcome back, Drake," and he reached out his hand to shake that of his brother-in-law.

The young man reciprocated the action before adding, "I'm sorry for your loss."

All Louis could do was give a nod of his head, as the pain was still too near for him, and the thought of him being crowned the following day was a maddening idea that he tried to keep at bay. As he drew his hand away, he took note of the leather glove on the sailor's hand. "That is a rather handsome glove you have there," the royal spoke.

"Thank you. It was my father's fencing glove."

"We shall have to test it out then," smiled the future king. "As soon as things calm down after the coronation, we shall have ourselves a duel."

A little laughter escaped Drake's mouth, before he replied. "Aye, your majesty."

Elizabeth then walked over to her daughter and took her hands. "Bella, as happy as I am to see you again, you both took a terrible risk in coming back home."

"Some risks are worth anything," smiled Drake, as he casually made his way over to the windows and closed the curtains. "Of course, doing anything to help make them less risky never hurt anyone," he laughed a bit with Izzy.

"Mother's right," started Louis, not joining in the laughter, but now feeling the weight of the situation. "Father did what he had to in order to cover up for you two running away together."

"I know, Louis, but I had to see you and Mother again, especially after hearing the news…" spoke Izzy, opening up her heart to her family.

The two royals looked at each other, knowing that Izzy was right, and they were both happy to see her again. "Louis, why don't you take them into your study, where you cannot be bothered. I will do my best in keeping the household staff busy for the day. Afterall, there is a lot that needs to be done before tomorrow's coronation."

Looking over at his mother, Louis knew how painful it was for her to sacrifice her time with her only daughter that she may never get to see again. However, he was also very grateful to be able to spend time with his sister. After a nod of his head, he turned his attention to the youngest couple in the room with a smile. "Follow me," and he led them out of the room and to his study, locking the door behind them.

Chapter Four

Of Memories and Stories

"… And that was when the vampires swooped out and captured me. They then flew me to the top of Mount Stoker and held me captive," explained Izzy in one of her tales, as Louis sat in a chair and Drake stood by the window in the young king's study.

"Why did they take you? Just because you landed on their land?" asked Louis, leaning forward, as he listened intently to the story.

"They just wanted her," smiled Drake, with his arms crossed, as he leaned against the curtains.

All Izzy could do was giggle. "For some strange reason, they wanted me to be their leader. I guess it was always my destiny to be a queen," she joked.

"But how did you escape?"

"I saved her, of course!" smirked Drake.

"Drake…" laughed Izzy, and Drake came over to wrap his arms around her and kiss her cheek. "Yes, Drake did save me. He remembered the crate of garlic we were bringing to Letuchavania. It seems they had a vampire issue as well," she added with a wink.

"Well, your sister was the brilliant one to realize that we could make garlic necklaces by attaching the bulbs to the twine that held the crate together. It made sure the vampires wouldn't come near us."

"But it wouldn't have been possible, if you hadn't spent all day pulling the crate up the mountain. I still can't believe how quickly you made it up the steep slope."

"Well, I had no choice. I had to make it up to you before nightfall when the vampires would awaken."

"It seems the two of you make a good pair," interjected Louis.

"When you love someone, anything is possible," spoke the young sailor with complete honesty, and he once again kissed his wife.

All the crowned prince could do was smile at his sister and brother-in-law and be content in their happiness. It was a moment later that a bitter sweet smile took over, as his mind thought back to times when his sister was gone. All his parents would talk about was hoping their daughter was joyful. "… Father would be overjoyed to see you so happy, Bella."

Izzy's smile started to shake, as a tear made its way to her eye. "I wish I was able to see him one more time."

"He was one of the most kind and honorable men that I had ever met," spoke up Drake, still keeping his arms around Izzy, but now it was to embrace her with comfort and support. "Not many kings, let alone men, would allow their daughter to run off for love and not force her to do what had been promised of her."

As Izzy ran her hand over the cheek that had just become damp, the thought once again occurred to her. She was not forced to return to complete the peace alliance between Dauphin Magie and Exousia. "Louis, how did Father manage to get out of the deal between us and King Theias?"

Louis stood up from his chair and made his way over to the window to see clouds starting to roll in and the wind picking up. "On the day you both ran off with each other, he proclaimed that the Princess of Dauphin Magie was lost at sea, and he made sure that everyone in the kingdom was informed of it," and as water filled his eyes, he looked back at his sister. "He took away the life you were born into so that you could have a brand new one. I know in my heart that it was one of the hardest decisions he had to make, because he knew that he would never see you again."

The former princess slowly took her husband's arms off from around her and stood up to go to her brother. She then hugged him and started to cry into his chest. "I'm so sorry, Louis. I didn't think my running away would bring so much pain to everyone."

Holding her close, Louis tried to bring a smile to his face, as he looked down at his baby sister in his arms. "It's alright, Bella. We were sad that we never got to say goodbye, but either way you would have left us that day. At least with Drake, we knew that you would be happy," and he smiled over at the renounced pirate, who returned the kind gesture back. It was then that the prince held out his right hand to his brother-in-law, who came over and accepted it in a firm shake. "Thank you taking good care of Bella."

"It's my pleasure, but there is one thing. She doesn't need anyone to take care of her," started Drake with a smile. "She's royalty and knows how to not only take care of herself but do the best she can for others."

"You don't have to be royalty to do that. You just have to be a good person."

"As flattering as it is hearing you both talk that way about me," started Izzy as she leaned back and wiped away her tears with her hands. "Could you both please stop talking about me as if I weren't in the room?"

"Sorry, Bella, but it's hard not to speak highly of you," and Louis released his embrace on his sister.

"He has a good point. Not everyone would give up living in a palace and having everything they want."

"If I recall correctly, you did the same thing, Drake," and Izzy sent a knowing smile in his direction.

All Drake could do was shrug his shoulders a bit. "What can I say? The seas were calling me and palace life was no place for a privateer."

"Well, it seems it was calling both of us," and she took a step back to stand in the middle between the two gentlemen in her life. "And right now, I'm just happy to be back with both of you by myside for the time being."

"And since it is still just the three of us," began Louis. "How about another story of one of the amazing adventures that you both shared?"

"Hmm… there's a lot of different adventures we've been on in the last three years…" pondered Drake. "But what's the most exciting one?"

"What about the Sea Sirens?" asked Izzy.

"No, all you did was put candle wax in my ears to keep me from jumping overboard. Besides, it feels like it's been told too many times."

"It's a good thing only men are vexed by them," giggled Izzy.

"Why is that?" asked the future king.

"You know… I don't know the answer to that. I guess they'd never encountered a woman before," shrugged Izzy.

"Well, isn't it a sailor's superstition that women were bad luck to have onboard a ship?" asked Louis. "Not that I paid much attention to it… nor have I gone sailing much."

"Aye, that it is, Louis," replied Drake. "That's why we don't sail with anyone but ourselves."

"If having a woman on board brought bad luck, then I'd say the hurricane we were pulled into definitely brought some truth out of that superstition," spoke up Izzy.

"Hurricane?" asked the perplexed prince, his eyes growing wide with worry.

"Well, it was more like a typhoon. I'm still shocked that our ship survived it," began Drake.

"That sounds like an adventure I would like to hear. Do you mind sharing, Bella?" asked Louis, as he took a seat, as anxious as a young child awaiting a bed time story.

"I would love to, but Drake can spin a far better yarn than I ever could," smiled Izzy, as she took her seat back to leave her husband standing in front of the descendants of royal blood.

The buccaneer then took center stage, pondering on how he would tell the tale that almost cost the married couple their lives. Before starting, he let his eyes drift to the window where the wind was starting to howl and the sky was black with no sign of starlight, as he began to twist his hands with one another. "It was a dark and stormy night, much worse than what we are experiencing. Izzy and I were on our small Cutter, making way for the band of trading isles when suddenly the wind picked up speed and hail the size of doubloons started falling from the sky..."

∞ ∞ ∞

Chapter Five

Dolus' Ring

"Keep a steady hand on the wheel!" called out Drake, as he tried to pull in the sails, so they would not be torn to pieces by the hail.

"I'm trying my best! She keeps wanting to get out of my hands!" shouted back Izzy, desperately trying to keep the wheel from spinning out of control.

Getting pounded by the mix of rain and hail, Drake finally managed to tie the ropes to the mast and hoped his sailor's knot was good enough to hold. He then raced towards the helm, but was knocked into the Starboard side by a giant wave coming off the Port. It took him a moment, but with a shake of his head to get the wet hair out of his face, he was able to regain his stance and make his way to the ship's Aft. When another wave threatened to swoop down, he went up behind the young girl. Drake put his hands over the frightened girl's hands to try to shield her, as much as possible, and not let her wash overboard. "Izzy, are you alright?"

The soaked girl looked up into her husband's emerald eyes, scared and in pain from the pelting of the weather. She had not been at sea for very long, so this storm had her, understandably, scared to death. “I… I’m…” she could not get the words out, for the pain at her throat was unbearable.

“Get below deck and stay in our quarters, away from the windows,” he ordered, knowing that this was too much for her to handle.

“No!” Izzy managed to blurt out, despite the pain it caused her. “I’m staying up here with you.”

“It’s not safe!”

“Wherever you go, I go!” she called back and then took an enlarged piece of hail to the side of her face, just missing her eye.

“Izzy!” screamed Drake, as he let go of the wheel to put both of his hands on her face to try to get a better look at it. There was blood coming down over her cheek, as her eyes tried to close. “Izzy, you have to stay with me! Don’t fall asleep!” He kept trying to shake her, but a familiar noise drew his attention away from his wife. The sailor looked over his shoulder with wide eyes to see a typhoon sized wave about to engulf their ship. With not a moment to spare, he pulled himself and Izzy back into a small corner behind the helm, leading down into the belly of the ship, and held his wife close. With one last breath drawn, everything went black.

Opening her eyes, Izzy looked around the misty land. Her body ached from being tossed around so much, and she noticed she had a few cuts where her clothes were torn. Nothing looked familiar to her, and it took a few moments to even fathom what had happened before. “Dra- Drake…” she got out with a scratchy voice.

It took a few minutes, but the royal turned sailor was finally able to stand up and try to have a better look around. Nothing was in sight, not even wood chips from what should have been a wreckage. All that she could see was a sickly green mist that just barely covered the land and half dead palm trees. "Drake!" Izzy tried calling out again, to no avail. She then dragged her leg behind her, stumbling to walk away from the sea.

The young lass attempted to navigate the island for what seemed like hours, however due to her condition, Izzy was not able to cover much land before falling in a heap at a pair of sandals before her. Her eyes slowly looked up at the owner of the footwear to see a young, glowing face and long honey hair that cascaded along grey dress robes. In the hand of the fair maiden was a pomegranate. "Let me help you, my dear," spoke a voice that seemed unworldly, as a fragile hand was extended out to the girl on the ground.

Izzy cautiously looked at the hand before reaching out to accept it and slowly stand on her good leg. She then reached for a tree trunk to rest her weight against, as she stood in slight awe of the lady that seemed to be descended from immortals. "Who are you?" the female sailor finally asked, her voice still frail.

With a shake of her head, the lady responded. "It does not matter. Let me see your injury," and the angelic woman leaned over to look at Izzy's leg. Then before Izzy could say anything, she felt an otherworldly pain running through her injured leg, as the lady lay her hand on it. Finally, with a gasp rushing out of the young girl's mouth, the pain was gone, and the former princess could stand on it again. Words again were stopped before escaping Izzy's mouth when the lady spoke up, "There now. You should have no further trouble."

"...Thank you," finally left Izzy's lips before her eyes closed again. There were so many things clouding her mind, as if a storm blew them all in at once. Pain and suffering seemed to be taking a toll on her, but she could not explain why. It was as if a storm rolled in to bring all of her devastating memories to the surface.

"Your mind seems troubled. May I offer you some help?" Upon hearing those words, Izzy began to nod her head, fervently, as tears burned her eyes for reasons she could not explain. "Here," and the lady held out her hand containing the pomegranate. "Just eat this and it will put your mind at ease."

As she reached out for the deceitful fruit, a voice screamed "IZZY! DON'T!" And before she could turn her head to see the owner of the voice, Drake reached out and swatted the fruit away before it could touch her hand.

"You foolish boy! You deny her peace?"

Drake looked the lady dead in the eye as he spoke. "She doesn't need any peace that you offer her! Love is more powerful and will grant her peace."

"Fine! See if your 'love' can help you pass my test to escape the Ring," and with those words, the mysterious woman vanished in the mists.

Breathing hard, the sailor looked down on his wife, who was now on the ground. He then kneeled next to Izzy and put his arms around her. "Are you alright?"

"I… I think so…" she was able to get out, as her clouded mind was now clearing up.

The former pirate then pulled her closer, grateful that they had both survived, but he thought long and hard on what their test could be.

"Drake, are you alright?"

Snapping his eyes open, he looked down at the worried woman in his arms. Those words pierced his thoughts. "Aye… I'll be fine," and he leaned her up. "We need to figure out what this test is and get out of here. Follow me," and Drake took ahold of her hand, before leading them towards the beaches.

"I'm sure everything will be just…" and the royal's gaze drifted to the side. "…Fine…" Her eyes then widened at what she beheld. "Mary?"

Drake then turned his attention in the same direction as his wife's, and he was astounded to behold the ghostly image of Izzy's former lady in waiting. "It cannot be…" he uttered, as he started to move forward.

"Drake…"

The young captain stopped dead in his tracks at the voice that uttered his name. He had not heard that voice in years, and it had only become a distant dream. "Dad?"

∞ ∞ ∞

"Mary? Is that really you?" questioned the young lady, as she stepped towards the specter. The apparition nodded her head before the girl continued. "How is this possible?"

"Persephone," Mary whispered, and Izzy looked at her quizzically. "She made a deal with Dolus. He set up this island as a trap to for sailors. Once you enter Dolus' Ring, you cannot leave. The goddess took pity on the mortals, so she struck a deal with him that is they passed a test, they had three hours to escape the island. Each person's test is different."

"Why only three hours though?"

Mary looked away from her friend, and she began to run her fingers overs the vegetation that grew on the island as she answered. "Cerberus. One hour for each head he has, as he is the guard at the entrance of the Underworld. You must pass him to escape that realm, and thus a sailor must pass the stormy seas that keep them separated from their freedom as well."

All Izzy could do was stand there and look at her friend, after hearing what she was up against. However, she soon started to realize something: she was acting the same way that she did the last time that she saw Mary. Why could she only put her needs before her friend's needs? True, Izzy did try to help, but when she comprehended that it was too late, she quickly moved on. It had always bothered her. Even now, all she was doing was trying to find a way to help herself. The pain of guilt struck her more than it had ever done before.

Moments ticked by, as the sound of silence filled the air surrounding the two ladies. The stillness was only interrupted when Izzy finally found her voice and spoke, "I'm sorry, Mary."

Taking a deep breath, Mary stopped in her tracks before she turned around to face the girl she had always watched over. "There is no need to apologize, Bella. You did as I had told you to do," and she walked over to the now older girl and took her hand in her own.

A tear began to stream down Izzy's cheek, as she turned her gaze to the ground, ashamed to look at her former best friend. "No, I should have saved you. You should still be alive. But what worse is…" and Izzy choked on her sobs as she continued. "… I didn't even give you a second thought after I realized you were gone. I was so focused on myself… and I'm ashamed of that."

"Bella," began Mary, as she pulled her into a hug. "It's all right. You couldn't have saved me. You did what you had to do in order to survive. That's all that I could ever ask for."

Izzy just closed her eyes, comforted by her friend's words. For the first time in many years, her mind and heart were at peace. A smile then came to her lips, as a thought entered her mind. She then leaned back and looked at Mary with a knowing smile. "I also wanted to say that you were right."

"About what?" replied Mary with a smile.

"Drake and I seeing each other again."

"I can see that," and the two girls started to laugh a little at the obvious joke.

"He saved my life that day and gave up what was most important to him for me," started Izzy. "And now we're married."

Mary's smile grew bigger, hearing the good news. "I had a feeling he would be the one for you, Bella. Now, did you do as I asked, and write down all of your adventures the two of you have shared in my present I gave you?"

Izzy reached into her pocket and pulled out the small journal that she was given on her eleventh birthday. "It's getting pretty full now. I may need another one soon."

"Well, that one you will have to get on your own," and the two friends continued their laughter.

∞ ∞ ∞

"Drake… Look at you, Son," spoke up Captain Black Spot Jack, as he put his hands on his son's shoulders. "Look at the fine man you've become."

"Dad…" and the teary-eyed young man could not resist anymore, as he wrapped his arms around his father. "I've missed you so much."

"I've missed you too," the old sailor whispered, as he pulled his son into a tight hug. "But, I am so proud of you."

Drake then leaned back to look into his father's eyes, with tears still in his own. "Proud of me? How can you be proud of me? I've let you down… and I'm so sorry I did," and he pulled away and turned his back towards the spirit.

The former captain then put his hand on his son's shoulder and squeezed it compassionately. "Drake, you have nothing to be sorry for."

"But… I handed over the Tesoro," and the young sailor refused to turn around and face the man he most admired.

"To Bilge Rat Bill, who was a great choice!"

"I still gave it up!" Drake finally screamed, trying to keep from going into full blown hysterics, and he took a few steps forward to put some distance between the two.

"Why did you give up the vessel?" Jack finally asked with an even voice.

Trying to gather his strength, Drake took several deep breaths to try to get his mind set back on track. He had let it become clouded with guilt, in which it had gotten the best of his emotions. "… To save Izzy."

"Was she worth it?"

After a moment, the young sailor turned and looked his father straight in the eye. "That and an entire armada."

A smile came to the old captain's lips, as he stepped over towards his son. "Love, especially true love, will always be worth more than planks of wood put together," and he then pulled Drake in to whisper in his ear. "You owe me no apology. All that you owe me is to see you happy with your lass. Do what you can to show that you love her, and if she loves you in return, she will do the same."

Drake smiled and then looked up to see Izzy and Mary walking towards them. "She already has," he whispered to his father before addressing the two ladies with a smile. "Hello, Izzy. Mary."

"Hello, Drake. It is good to see you again," spoke Mary with a nod of her head.

The young sailor then broke away from his father and stepped towards the two young women. "I am so sorry that I was the cause of your death. It should have never happened."

"You are forgiven. I know you didn't know it was our ship when you attacked."

"And you must be Izzy," interrupted the old captain, as he addressed the young lass, and she curtsied to him. "No need for formalities. I just wanted to thank you for taking care of my son."

"We take care of each other," smiled Izzy, as she took Drake's hand.

"Speaking of taking care of each other, we need to find a way off this island," spoke up Drake.

"Well, you completed the first task," Black Spot Jack stated.

Izzy and Drake had confused looks on their faces, and Drake finally found the words to speak on both of their behalves. “What do you mean we completed the first task? We didn’t do anything.”

“You both were able to face the guilt that has filled your hearts for so long and learned that you did not need to carry such a burden,” replied Mary. “Now you may return with a clear conscience, but you must escape within three hours.”

“But, it’s impossible,” spoke up Izzy.

“Bella,” started Mary. “You of all people should know that nothing is impossible, if you have the courage and compassion to pursue what you want most.”

The young girl then felt a squeeze of her own hand and looked over at her husband. “I’d do anything to keep you safe, Izzy.”

With a deep breath, the former princess then replied, “Then let’s make haste. Time is not on our side,” and when she turned to face the spirits to thank them, they were gone just as quickly as they had appeared.

∞ ∞ ∞

As fast as their feet would let them, they ran back to the beach, following their footprints to not get lost. They knew that the three hours would pass in the blink of an eye, and they could not afford to waste even a second. Their tiny vessel was sitting in the water, as if it had never been touched, and the pair raced on board to make sail. The only problem was the winds were very strong and would keep pushing them into the spit of land.

“Drake, how are we going to avoid the winds?”

The fledgling captain looked around, as his hair danced in front of his eyes. Everything seemed hopeless until he was able to catch a glimpse of Polaris, the brightest star in the sky. It could be seen shinning bright in a tiny patch that seemed to be the eye of the storm circling not too far behind them. “If we can manage to get underneath the eye when it reaches us, we should be able to safely sail out under the star’s watch,” he called out to Izzy.

“What do you need me to do, Drake?”

“Just hang on!” and he waited for the opportune moment, as his wife clung onto the railing. “Another moment…” Drake then uttered, as he had his hands on the helm to keep it steady. Just as the eye moved into position, he was able to turn the helm hard to Starboard, He then safely steered his ship into the calmness of the storm and eventually out into open waters far away from Dolus’ Ring.

Chapter Six

The Truth

"… It was many hours before we saw sunlight and clear seas again. That was when I knew we were finally safe for the time being," finished Drake, with Louis sitting on the edge of his seat, and Izzy moving her hand to brush away a tear that threatened to fall at the memory of seeing the apparitions.

"So, you both were able to make peace with the deceased?" asked Louis, still in shock.

Drake just nodded his head, gravely, as he started twisting his hands nervously with one another. "I don't think either of us were ready for that, and I can't speak for your sister, but I am grateful I was able to sort things out with my father." Drake then closed his eyes and took a deep breath, as he clenched his hands together to stop them from moving anymore.

"And I'm grateful to know that Mary does not blame me for not immediately mourning over her that day. Trust me, I did lots of mourning over the years that followed."

Louis just took a deep breath and thought over what the late King Philip would have said to him, if he were in the same situation. He figured it would have been words of comfort to remind him that he would be a good ruler. The words that his father last spoke to him, rang through his head, and they were words of wisdom to remind him that no matter what, he should always trust his heart. In this very moment, his heart was full at just seeing the sight of his sister once more. "I'm happy I at least am able to speak with the both of you and not your spirits," he spoke with a smile, trying to change the topic.

A smile came to Izzy's face, as she moved closer to her brother and put her arms around him. "I'm just happy to see you again," and before another beat could pass, she added in, "Now, let's discuss your coronation tomorrow."

"Aye! That's got to be the biggest party that you have ever thrown," added in Drake, finally releasing his hands, but moving his right hand into his pocket.

The future king took notice of the sailor's movement in his hands, but decided not to bring up the small distraction. "Well, the ceremony will take place when the sun is at it's highest in the sky, and then we will all have a moment to breathe before the ball at sunset. Very simple, nothing out of the ordinary. I don't want to be known as a ruler to waste our greatest assets. I want the people to know that I will be the ruler, who takes care of them, like Father did," explained Louis, his voice growing solemn.

"I don't think you have to worry about the kingdom thinking any less of you. They have known you and our family all of our lives. I truly believe you have their trust," encouraged Izzy.

A smile came to Louis' face, as he heard his sister's kind words. "I just wish there was a way for the both of you to attend both events."

After a few moments of quiet, Drake spoke up, thoughtfully, as he moved his hand from his pocket to his chin. "Maybe there is."

"How?" asked Louis, and Izzy also looked in the direction of the seafarer.

"On the ship, we use telescopes to see things from far away. If there was a way that we could be in a place overlooking the ceremony, we could watch it through our telescopes that we keep on ourselves," the sailor explained.

"You know, that could work. The ceremony is being held in the courtyard, and my study looks right down on it. Both of you could stay in here, and I'll see to it that no one enters the room until I return. With the curtains drawn, no one would be the wiser," Louis thought aloud, as he paced the floor and looked in the direction of the window with the curtains drawn shut. He then came to a stop and looked back at the couple. "What about the ball though?"

Izzy and Drake looked at each other, and within moments both of their eyes lit up, as they both had the exact same idea. "On our journeys visiting different kingdoms, we were able to see various types of parties thrown," began Izzy. "One of my favorites that we came across was called a masquerade. People would wear masks to conceal their identities during the party and dress up. They were fun, because we were able to meet lots of new people and learn so much more about them. It truly is amazing how truthful people are when no one knows who you are."

"It also helped us to enjoy areas that people might have recognized us in," added in Drake, once again moving his right hand back into his pocket. "Between your sister being a formal royal, and myself a former privateer for the king of Valiaguila, we had to keep low profiles."

"Then it is settled!" started Louis. "I will have the castle seamstress create enough masks to hand out to the guests tomorrow. Then I will have the household staff hand them out to the guests, as they depart the coronation ceremony and explain what we shall be doing at the ball," explained the royal, as a grin came to his face. "We may even have a new tradition for Dauphin Magie!"

"I'm so happy we'll be able to attend!" cried out Izzy, as she hugged her brother.

A bright grin came onto Drake's face, so happy for his family, that he pulled his hand out from his pocket and went to extend it out to Louis. His hand then visibly shook, and he pulled it back into a fist, before sliding it behind his back. He then turned his gesture into a slight bow of acknowledgement. "This will surely be a time to be treasured by all."

The ruler to be took note of all of the gestures his brother-in-law made, since telling the story of the escape of Dolus' Ring. And despite discussing the plans for his coronation day, Louis still had something nagging at the back of his mind, and it would drive him insane if he did not ask the burning question. "Bella, could you do me a favor and read over the speech I prepared for tomorrow? You were always far better at drafting speeches than I was."

"Of course, Louis," smiled Izzy, and she moved over to her brother's desk to read over his long-prepared speech for the commencement.

"Drake, can I see you for a moment?" asked Louis, and he ushered his brother-in-law to the side. "You left out part of that story, didn't you?"

After several moments of silence, the younger boy nodded his head and looked down shamefully. "How did you know?"

"I noticed you kept moving your hands about, as if you had a secret," replied Louis, and Drake bit his lower lip. "What really happened?"

The sailor took a deep breath, and kept his voice hushed. He kept his head pointed at a downwards angle, as he returned to the story. "When Persephone was offering the pomegranate to your sister…"

As the young girl reached out for the deceitful fruit, a voice screamed "IZZY! DON'T!" And before she could turn her head to see the owner of the voice, Drake reached out and grabbed the fruit before it could touch her hand.

"You foolish boy! You know the price at which it has just cost you?"

Drake looked the lady dead in the eye, as he spoke. "I'm willing to pay it."

"Pass my test to escape the Ring, and you will pay it," and with those words, the mysterious woman vanished in the mists.

Breathing hard, the sailor looked down on his wife, who was now on the ground, as he let the fruit roll out of his hand. He then kneeled next to Izzy and put his arms around her. "Are you alright?"

"I… I think so…" she was able to get out, as her clouded mind was now clearing up.

The former pirate then pulled her closer, grateful that they had both survived. Moving his right hand, he could not help but peer at his palm. Seven seed imprints now lay on his stained hand, and all he could do was make a fist to hide it from the world, as he closed his eyes. He only thought of what was now at hand and what the future would hold for him.

"Drake, are you alright?"

Snapping his eyes open, he looked down at the worried woman in his arms. Those words pierced his thoughts. "Aye... I'll be fine," and he leaned her up. "We need to figure out what this test is and get out of here." Taking ahold of her hand, Drake began to lead them towards the beaches. He tried so hard to set his mind straight and not think on what had just happened. It was then that he felt a squeeze on his hand and turned his head to look back at Izzy.

"Something is wrong. Tell me the truth, Drake," and she stood there waiting on an answer.

Mustering up the best smile he could, Drake lied. "I'm just worried about what our test will be."

Izzy decided she would ignore his lie for the time being. She knew him all to well to know when he was telling the truth and when he was not, and now was the time to not further press the matter. However, there was some truth in his words, as they did not know what the test would be and how to complete it. "I'm sure it will be just..." and the royal's gaze drifted to the side. "...Fine..."

All Drake could do was look away with closed eyes. No other living person had heard the true tale up until this point, and he never thought he would reveal it. It was only a moment before he felt someone take his right hand, and he looked over to see Louis turning his palm face up, taking off his glove, and looking at the imprints that now scarred the flesh.

"It's as if you have seven tiny black spots on your hand," whispered the future king.

"I know," replied Drake with an even tone and eyes that had lost all warmth and become quite serious.

Catching his gaze, the two gentlemen exchanged a silent acknowledgement that this version of the story was to remain a secret from all, especially Izzy. Of course, now that Louis had heard the true tale, he had another question that plagued his mind. "How did you keep my sister from the true story?"

Taking a deep breath, Drake lowered his eyes in shame. "You know how the more times a story is told; the more people remember the version that they heard the most?" and Louis nodded his head. "Since her mind was already clouded at the moment that I intervened with Persephone, I was able to alter the details little by little. On many calm nights, we would sit out on the deck and tell stories of our favorite adventures. I kept choosing that one for many reasons. One of them being to remind ourselves that we were forgiven of our guilt involving Mary and my father. It's easy to get lost in bad memories and only focus on the negative. By reminding ourselves of the forgiveness, we turned it into a positive experience and put our minds a little more at ease. However, because I kept bringing it up, I had to slowly change that part of the story to keep her blinded to the truth."

Louis glanced over Drake's shoulder to see his sister still reading over his speech then back down at the sailor's palm. "Why won't you tell Bella? I know she would want to know."

With a shake of his head, Drake replied, "I can't. Your sister means more to me than anything. I won't have her worried over me. She has enough on her mind," and Louis nodded his head in agreement. "Promise you won't tell her."

"I promise," responded Louis, and Drake slid the glove back on to his hand.

∞ ∞ ∞

Chapter Seven

The Glove

A star filled sky graced the kingdom of Dauphin Magie, and watched over all who slept, except one, who was seeking asylum in its peacefulness. The maniac storm had let up shortly after the couple had finished speaking with the future king, and it left behind a peaceful night. Drake sat on the same bench in the open window that he did when he was just twelve years old. As he watched the night sky, his mind floated along different memories. Before long, he was soon yanking at his glove and slowly pulled it off. Those seven tiny black spots creeped their way into his mind, once again, and all he could think about was his time in Dolus' Ring and his father's looks of fear at the markings.

"Why did you give up the vessel?" Captain Black Spot Jack asked with an even voice.

Trying to gather his strength, Drake took several deep breaths to try to get his mind set back on track. He had let it become clouded with guilt, in which it had gotten the best of his emotions. "... To save Izzy."

"Was she worth it?"

After a moment, the young sailor turned and looked his father straight in the eye. "That and an entire armada. I would do anything to save her-" and the boy gasped in pain, as he reached with his left hand to grip his right hand.

"Drake, what's wrong?" asked the former captain with concern, as he took a step forward.

"Nothing... it's nothing," quietly responded Drake, as he pulled his arm away to hide his hand.

"Let me see your hand," and the old seaman reached out to take his son's hand in his own. A gasp then left his mouth, as he saw the seven black spots imprinted in his son's palm. "Drake...."

"I had to, Dad. Persephone was offering death to Izzy, and I couldn't let her take it."

"You know what the Black Spot means, Drake."

Closing his eyes, Drake nodded his head solemnly. "I'm prepared to take whatever punishment Persephone has for me. I just can't let Izzy know. I don't want her to worry."

Black Spot Jack looked down for a moment, thinking over what his son had just stated, and how much courage it took to put someone else's wellbeing ahead of their own. He then reached into his pocket and pulled out a black leather glove. "Well... if you're going to keep this secret, you will need something to hide those markings," and he handed the glove over to his son.

"But, Dad... this is your's. You've had it for as long as I can remember."

"I picked up that glove the day I met your mother, and it's never left my side since... well... until today. I want you to

have it, Drake. Whenever you look at it, think of your mother and me, and think of the sacrifices you are making for your wife."

"Thank you, Dad. It means everything to me that you'll help me keep this secret to protect Izzy. I'm just sorry I couldn't protect everything that you loved."

A smile came to the old captain's lips, as he stepped over towards his son. "Love, especially true love, will always be worth more than planks of wood put together," and he then pulled Drake in to whisper in his ear. "You owe me no apology. All that you owe me is to see you happy with your lass for as long as that may be. Do what you can to show that you love her, and if she loves you in return, she will do the same."

Drake smiled and then looked up to see Izzy and Mary walking towards them. "She already has," he whispered to his father.

Knock. Knock.

Snapping his head up at the sound from the other side of the door, the sailor quickly slipped his glove back on before standing up. If there was one thing that could pull him out of his reminiscing, it was the knowledge of making sure his father's glove kept his secret from his wife. After turning his head to make sure Izzy was still asleep, he made his way over towards the door and opened it. "Sir Arthur? What brings you here this late at night?" asked the surprised boy.

"His majesty wished for me to give these to you," spoke Arthur, with no emotion to his voice, as he handed over two colorfully ordained masks to the former pirate. "He was very pleased with the masquerade idea, and he wanted to know if you had acquired the telescopes for the ceremony in the morning."

"Aye, I slipped down to the docks after speaking with him, and I was able to get both telescopes for the two of us."

"Very well," started the elder. "Once the palace is clear, I will escort the two of you to the future king's study for viewing. There will be two guards placed at the doorway to make sure no one enters," and Arthur turned to go.

"Wait!" called out Drake, in a hushed voice, as not to disturb anyone, and Arthur turned around. "I have never sincerely apologized for what happened to your daughter, Sir Arthur," and the older gentleman lowered his head. "Mary was a wonderful person, and I never intended to harm her in any way, nor you. I have Mary's forgiveness, and I must ask for your's. I know it is a lot to ask, and you have every right not to forgive me. But, please know I never would have attacked that ship, had I known it was of the Kingdom of Dauphin Magie. After re-uniting with my father, I told him of the kindness of this amazing kingdom, and he agreed to never attack ships that flew Dauphin Magie's colors again. That day I attacked the ship of the princess, there were no flags that were being flown, and I thought it fair game among pirates. So, please know that I never intended ill will on anyone on that ship. Had I known, I would have sailed on, and we probably would have never met again. If you can find it in your heart, I do ask your forgiveness."

A tear sprang to the royal advisor's eye that he could not hide, hearing all of what the young man, who took his princess and daughter away from him, spoke to him. Deep down, he knew Drake was a noble as the bravest knight, but the thought of his daughter dying at his hand, was like a dagger to his heart. "I… I forgive you…" he choked out. "No matter what happened, my last moment with Mary, was the last moment I knew I was going to have with my daughter, as she was bound to the ship that was to take Princess Isabella away forever. The only reason we have been able to see Bella more, was because of what you did, and I never was able to thank you for bringing her happiness that she would not have seen in Exousia."

Moving his gloved hand, Drake gripped Arthur's shoulder in compassion. As difficult as it was to speak of that dark day, they both knew in their hearts that good came from such a massacre. "Thank you…"

A silent, understanding nod passed from Arthur to Drake, before he turned to leave. It was only when Drake retreated into the room that he heard, "Have a good night," before turning back to acknowledge and finding no one there. He then returned to his old room and closed the door to not attract any unwanted attention.

Several moments later he placed the two masks down on the dresser in the room, before turning his attention to his wife once more. Today had been the most he had discussed the events that happened the day that he and Izzy entered Dolus' Ring than ever before. After speaking the truth to Louis, Drake found he could not get those memories out of his head. The more he tried to escape them, the harder they pressed their way through. Now looking at Izzy, all he could picture was the events following after their escape.

Captain Drake stood out on the deck of the little ship, looking off into the distance at the swirling storms that circled Dolus' Ring. His mind was a whirlwind to the equivalent of what he saw from what he had just experienced. All he could do was try to focus on what had just happened, as he played with the black leather glove on his hand.

"Drake?"

The young man slowly turned around to see his wife behind him. She appeared to still be shaken up by the whole experience. "What is it, Izzy?" he asked quietly.

"How did you get that?" she asked, as she motioned to the glove on his hand.

Almost instantly, the young man pulled his hand back towards himself, as if to hide the gloved appendage. It took him a moment to realize that Izzy had no idea what was hiding under the fabric that was dark as night, and he was able to take a deep breath and close his eyes before responding. "My father gave it to me to remember him and my mother by. He found this the day he met my mother and had always kept it on him. When we spoke, he gave it to me to keep for luck." Drake figured telling a version of the truth was better than lying to the person he trusted most.

A smile came to Izzy's lips, as she stepped over towards her husband and took the gloved hand in her own. "I'm glad you have a piece of your parents with you. It's truly sweet how your father cared for your mother, and I'm glad you were able to spend time with him once more."

"Me too, Izzy. Me too," and he put his other arm around her to pull her into a hug, so that she could not see the pain of his heartache on his face.

"As long as I'm around, I will make sure you are taken care of. I promise," softly spoke the seafarer, as he sat down on the bed beside the sleeping princess and slipped off into his dreamland.

∞ ∞ ∞

Chapter Eight

Louis' Ball

"I'm so glad you both could be here," spoke Louis to his sister and brother-in-law. They were just outside of the ballroom, enjoying their time together before the real festivities would begin and all of the attention the new king would embrace.

"Me too!" exclaimed Izzy, as she hugged her brother.

"Thanks for making this a masquerade for us," said Drake, as he adjusted his mask to be able to see a bit better.

"Of course! I didn't want to risk ruining Bella's marriage, and we needed the whole family together again. And thank you both for the suggestion. I haven't seen this many people excited over something new since you taught them how to do a 'jig'," and the two men laughed, as the young girl kept a bittersweet smile on her face, thinking back to the last ball with the entire family together.

"I just wish Father were here," replied Izzy with a tear in her eye.

Louis put his hands on his sister's shoulders and looked her straight in her eyes. "He would be so proud of you, Bella."

"Was he suffering?"

The newly crowned king turned his back on the couple, not able to speak the truth to his sister's distraught face. "The last few weeks were hard. His strength was failing, and my training with him almost feels like a blur now. On the night of his-" and Louis had to take a breath, as the memory was too vivid. "- When the castle staff came to my study… I just knew. He was so weak," and the young man turned back around to face the sailors. "… But I don't think he suffered."

Tears started streaming down the lass' face, as she thought about what that night must have been like for her brother. As much as she had wished that she had been there, she also knew that she probably would not have been able to handle the grief in the room. Saying goodbye to someone you love for the final time is the most pain a heart could ever endure, and even for some people, it is too much to take. Knowing that you will never see them again is like sailing on the sea, constantly in a drift with nothing but the vast ocean surrounding you.

"Izzy, are you alright?"

Those words pulled the former royal back into reality from her thoughts. She had been so deep in them that it was almost as if she were in her father's room that dark night. "Aye… yes, I'm fine."

Drake then moved his hands to dry the tears that stained her cheeks. "I know it's hard, Izzy, but he would not want you to be sad. Believe me. I know," he said with a reassuring smile.

Hearing what her husband said brought clarity to her mind. Drake had lost both of his parents long ago, and after meeting his ghostly father, she knew his words were right. It would always be a pain that will never leave, but she could not let grief take over her life. "You're right. Besides, we're here to celebrate Louis tonight," she added with a smile.

"Huzzah to that!" chimed in Drake, as he punched his gloved fist above his head.

"Then what are we waiting for? Let's have some fun! We have been doing the 'jig' at all of our balls since you taught Bella, Drake," spoke Louis, as he ushered his family into the great ballroom, where everyone was dancing. "Like I said, everyone loves it."

All Drake and Izzy could do was laugh at the comment, but deep-down Drake was looking forward to dancing the jig again on dry land. His excitement only grew as he heard the tempo of the music pick up even more, and he took his wife's hands and led her in a dance around the room. The whole room was laughing and smiling, as each and every person participated.

It was only when the music ended that everyone in attendance applauded the musicians and King Louis stepped forward. "I wanted to thank you all for coming here in our time of sadness and celebration. It is hard to believe my father, King Philip, passed away just over six months ago, and it is even harder to think I am standing here before you. He was a great king, and I can only hope to be half the ruler that he was," and Louis had to pause to catch his shaky voice from becoming apparent. "If he were standing here right now, I know he would like to thank everyone for their support… but tell us not to be sad. There was only one time… that I know he was ever truly saddened… but thinking of happiness, he was able to move on," and Louis looked right at Izzy, as tears burned in the girl's eyes. "So, I raise a toast to my father and Dauphin Magie!" and Louis raised his goblet.

"Cheers," spoke the entire room, as they too raised their glasses in a toast. That is, all but one person.

"Izzy," uttered Drake, as he turned to see his wife hasten out of the room in tears.

∞ ∞ ∞

Exiting the room and turning around a corner, the sailor found the young girl crying into a drapery. "Izzy… Are you alright?"

"No!" she cried. "It's not fair!"

"I know it's not," spoke Drake, as he went to embrace her.

Almost immediately after he put his arms around her, Izzy pushed Drake away. "Get away from me. It's your fault we're here!"

Drake tried to keep his composure, knowing that this was the grief that was talking. "I'm sorry, Izzy. I didn't know he had died when I suggested we go to Papillon de Baleine. If I had, I wouldn't have suggested it."

Not able to control her breathing through the sobs and wanting to just dry her face, Izzy ripped off her mask and threw it at the ground. "I know… I know…" she barely got out, as she looked away for a few moments. "I'm sorry, Drake. I…" and her lips kept quivering so hard, it was near impossible to get out. She tried taking a deep breath to focus her mind. "I just never got to say goodbye…"

A thousand phrases wanted to be expressed by the former pirate, but he was afraid if he had said anything, it would make the matter worse. Instead, he tried once more to just take her hand and squeeze it to let her know that she had someone that she could trust and to always be there for her.

It was with this simple gesture that the poor girl just looked up into her husband's eyes and knew that she could be completely open with him no matter what. "I miss my daddy…" she barely got out, before wrapping her arms around Drake and sobbing into his shoulder, and all he could do was hold her and let her cry.

∞ ∞ ∞

The couple, however, was not aware that in the shadows was a tall, thin man, who had witnessed the whole ordeal. He made no sound, as he disappeared deeper into the shadows with the secret that would soon change everyone's lives.

Chapter Nine

Terms

"Excuse me, your highness," spoke Arthur, as he entered Louis' study.

The king looked up from the parchments that covered his desk. Even though he had been studying under his father for most of his life and his coronation happened the day before, he still did not feel as if he were ready to be King of Dauphin Magie. "What is it, Sir Arthur?"

"It is the Kingdom of Exousia. King Theias and Prince Adonis request to have an audience with you."

Louis took a deep breath before returning his attention down at the documents before him. "Tell them we will arrange for something-"

"Immediately," interrupted Arthur.

Hearing his advisor speak before he could finish his thought truly caught the young king off guard. "How serious is this?" he questioned with a solemn tone.

"Judging from their royal advisor's tone, we should not postpone this meeting any longer than we already have."

Closing his eyes, Louis took a deep breath and pondered on the words that his dearest friend and councilor just used. The royal knew that one day he would be called to hold an emergency meeting, but he did not expect it to be the day after he was crowned king. "Very well. I will see him shortly in the throne room."

"As you request, your majesty," and the advisor hastened out of the room, leaving Louis to wonder what the royals of Exousia wanted before making his way to the throne room.

∞ ∞ ∞

"Announcing their royal highnesses, King Theias and Prince Adonis of Exousia," introduced Arthur, as he stepped aside to let the two foreign royals into the throne room.

Louis slowly stood up from his throne and came down to greet the two gentlemen, as they entered. He kept a smile of dignity on, remembering that Theias was a friend of his father's and the two men had respected each other. "Good morning," started Louis with a nod of his head.

The father and son gave a slight bow, before the elder of the two spoke up. "Good morning, King Louis. Might I start off with off with offering my condolences on your father's passing."

"Thank you. He thought highly of you, King Theias."

Theias in turn nodded his head to acknowledge the compliment. "Please, Louis, let us set aside the formalities. We have, after all, known each other for the entirety of your life. In fact, I was one of the first to lay eyes on you, after you were born."

The comment put the young king more at ease, as the two kingdoms had always been close. "Of course, Theias."

"I am sorry to interrupt," began Arthur, stepping forward. "However, as his highness is newly crowned, he does have a lot of business to attend to. May we inquire as to the urgency of your audience, King Theias?"

"Of course, Sir Arthur. I do not want to take up too much of your time," began the visiting ruler. "Now, Louis, I hate to bring up another dark topic, given that your father's passing was only a few months ago, and I know it is still hurting, but I must know something. What happened to your sister?"

The question had completely blindsided the youngest in the room of royals. No one outside of the family had brought up the story that King Philip had addressed since within a year's time of Princess Isabella's supposed demise, and no one had ever raised question to the good king. In fact, of all the topics that could have been brought to light, that was the one that Louis thought he would never have to address again.

Seeing the trouble in Louis' eyes, Arthur stepped forward. "If you may permit me, your majesty, I shall recount it for you, as I know it is a difficult subject considering she was your sister," and Louis gave a slight nod of his head towards his most trustworthy companion. "As you know, King Theias, that our dear Princess Isabella was on her way to marry your son, when her ship was viciously attacked upon by Pirates. I, myself, even lost my daughter that day. We thought we had a glimmer of hope, and she had returned to us. However, we were ready to sail her back to you once more, but fraud played an evil game. It turned out to be an imposter, and our dear princess was truly gone and lost at sea. King Philip had never been so devastated, and the kingdom never truly healed after-" and Sir Arthur was cut off, as he felt a blade slice open his arm.

"In Exousia we execute liars."

Immediately drawing his sword, Louis stepped forward and held it up to the elderly, royal advisor of King Theias. "Guards!" called the king. "Sir Arthur has been injured!"

"Ophion, that was un-necessary," began Theias, as he stepped forward to intervene between the two. "I must apologize for Ophion's behavior, Louis. He insists on following the law to a T and never wavering from it."

Louis kept his eyes focused on the so called "family friend", trying to figure out what Exousia's game was. Clearly, they were up to something, and he did not want to lose his higher ground. His eyes only moved slightly, as he saw Arthur being tended to by one of the palace guards, and he tried to keep his mind focused on the matter at hand. "What do you want, Theias?" he questioned in an even tone without moving his sword.

"Only for an old accord to be honored."

Shifting his eyes over towards Prince Adonis for a moment, Louis had to remind himself not to let any emotions give away the truth. "We told you. Princess Isabella is *dead*," and he could feel his voice catch in his throat as that fateful word came to his lips: *dead*.

"Please allow me to counter-act that very idea," began Theias, and he turned to the slithering consultant, who seemed to have a grin on his face that stretched across the tight, thin skin. "Ophion, will you please share what you saw last night," and hearing those words, fear came to Louis' eyes.

Slowly the advisor began to slink about, as he pulled out his handkerchief and wiped the blood off of his dagger before he spoke. "After your speech last night, I stepped out of the crowded room and took note of two others, who did the same. It was a man and young woman, who was in hysterics after your speech. They were around your age," and the elderly man circled behind Louis, who had lowered his sword but still kept a tight grip on it. "I took note that your speech seemed to have upset the young girl, and as I was about to intervene, she took off her mask. My eyes did not deceive me, as I knew it to be Princess Isabella."

"Liar," spoke Louis through gritted teeth.

Ophion held up a finger to silence the ruler of Dauphin Magie, and after he wagged it in his face for a moment, he slowly pulled it back to join the other four in his fist. "I would have believed your story about another girl looking just like her and deceiving others, however, the young girl kept referring to King Phillip as "daddy". Also, it was apparent that they were trying to hide from the rest of the court… as if they kept a secret." Louis kept his mouth shut, trying not to reveal anything whether by word or body language. "Ah… I see we have caught the king in a trap that had been set up to fool the rest of the world. The only question is why?"

Trying not to breathe hard, Louis' mind ran raced around his head quickly trying to think up ways to get him out of this corner that he was trapped in. After a few moments, he finally closed his eyes and spoke. "Close the doors, and everyone leave us to discuss."

One by one, the confused guards filed out until it was just the royals and advisors left alone in the room, and the doors closed with a loud thud. "So, it is true?" asked Adonis, just as confused as his father, and Louis nodded.

"Why couldn't you just leave this family to grieve in peace?" confronted Arthur, stepping up and holding his wounded arm with his free hand.

"You can't grieve someone, who is still alive," smirked Ophion.

"What do you want?" questioned Louis, his teeth back to grinding each other.

Theias stepped forward. "Your father was a man of his word, and I hope you will be too. Many years ago, Isabella's hand was promised to Adonis in exchange for peace. We are hoping you will honor that agreement."

"No! I can't do that to my sister!" screamed Louis, forgetting all of his training and becoming a concerning brother.

"Louis, you have no choice," started Theias, as he tried to keep his composure. "You have to keep to the diplomatic agreement."

"What happens if I don't?" questioned the newly appointed king, his anger still about him.

"Then you will sentence your kingdom to death," intervened Ophion, and Louis looked over at the snaky man. "In accordance with the kingdoms of the seas, we will have no choice but to declare war on you for breaking your accord of peace. If you do not hand her over, there will be an Armada awaiting your doorstep."

Fear struck Louis, as his anger melted away and all of his emotions came to light with no turning back. "No… please," he began, tears starting to come to his eyes, as he turned to Adonis. "You can't do this to my sister. I beg of you, please leave and keep our secret."

"I'm sorry, Louis, but I have the royal bloodline of Exousia to think about," solemnly spoke Adonis, trying to avert his eyes for fear of guilt.

"Theias," started Louis, as he turned his attention to the father. "You just spoke of being friends with my father. Can't you imagine how hard it was on him to do the right thing for Bella's happiness and take the grievance on his own heart to never see her again?"

Before Theias could speak, Ophion interrupted. "We must think about what is best for both kingdoms and not the whims of one insignificant girl."

"That girl is my sister," hissed Louis, his anger starting to rise again.

"And worth no more than the very pets that you own," retorted Ophion, with a menacing grin.

"She's more important than anything to me," and Louis got in the advisor of Exousia's face.

"Than what is more important: your kingdom or your precious sister?" countered Ophion, as Louis got quiet. "We will give you until sunrise tomorrow to make your decision. Either Isabella is on the ship with me, as I get ready to sail back home, or upon my return, we will send war ships out to destroy Dauphin Magie."

"Please, King Theias, I beg of you. You know this is what my father would never want," pleaded Louis, as he fell to his knees before Theias.

King Theias looked down upon the boy that was at his feet. His heart told him one thing, but his mind spoke another. "Louis… we have to uphold the accord. I'm sorry. We have to return to Exousia now, but Ophion will stay behind and let us know of your decision," and he turned, opened the doors, and walked out with his son.

"You have until sunrise tomorrow, your majesty, otherwise we shall return on an occasion more disheartening than what befell upon you six months ago," spoke Ophion before he disappeared from the room.

"Arthur, what are we going to do?" cried Louis, looking up at his trusted companion, now very much a scared little boy.

The advisor slowly made his way over to his king and kneeled beside him. “I’m sorry, sire, but even I cannot give any advice on this one. There is only one person, who can decide this. You know in your heart that you must tell her.”

I can’t do this to Bella…”

Chapter Ten

A Decision

"I can't do this…" uttered Louis, as he paced in his study. He had been thinking over the decision that weighed on his shoulders most of the day. To force his sister to give up not only the life she loved, but the person whom she wanted to spend the rest of it with, or doom his kingdom and the thousands who lived there and looked up to him for safety and prosperity. It was a decision that no one should ever have to endure.

"Do what your heart tells you…"

He could hear those words, repeated time and time again by his mother and father, ringing in his head. What was the right thing? His heart was torn in two for the love of his kingdom and the love of his sister. "I can't choose!"

Knock. Knock.

"Louis, you wanted to see us?"

Like a bolt of lightning, the king's head flashed up at the sound of his sister's voice on the other side of the door. No, he could not make his decision. Not now. He needed more time, but he could not leave her or his brother-in-law waiting on the other side of the dense wood. “Come… come in,” he called, his voice once again catching in his throat.

The door slowly opened, as Izzy and Drake stepped in and closed the door behind them. “Louis, what’s going on? Mom seemed very upset when she came to us.”

Queen Elizabeth was the only person that Louis told of what had happened. He thought she would be able to give some sage advice, as she had been a ruler much longer than he had. Upon hearing the news, Louis could tell that his mother’s heart broke all over again. She had been enduring ill news for so long that her complex seemed to be as pale as her spirit had become. In fact, it was only seeing her daughter and Drake again that had brought some cheerfulness back into her life after King Philip had passed on. Now knowing that her daughter’s happiness could be taken away brought frailty to her heart. However, she tried not to show it as she spoke to Louis, “Do what your heart tells you.”

“Bella, you may want to sit down,” and Louis moved his chair around for Izzy to have a seat in.

As the young girl sat down, her heart started to fill with dread. “Oh my goodness... it’s bad news, isn’t it? I don’t think I can take any more bad news.”

“Whatever Louis has to tell us, I know we can face it together,” gently spoke Drake, as he kneeled down next to his wife and took her hand, trying to be encouraging.

“No… you won’t be able to.”

“What?” the couple asked in a surprised unison.

Louis slowly made his way over to them and kneeled down in front of the two. “King Theias knows.”

"Huh?" spoke the confused girl before looking into her brother's eyes and recognizing the truth. "What? No! How did he find out?"

"It seems his right-hand man, Ophion, stepped out of the ballroom shortly after my speech as well. Bella," and he took his sister's hand in his own. "He saw you without your mask on and heard what you told Drake."

"This cannot be happening…" she groaned with her head buried in her hands.

"Wait a moment," started Drake, interjecting. He was confused by one thing. "How does he know what she looks like? My understanding was this betrothal was made when she was eleven, and I know he was not on the ship that my crew destroyed when she was on her way to Exousia. She was the only survivor."

Standing up, Louis began to pace the room before he started thinking back to the times that his whole family lived together. "Shortly after you left, Drake, Father announced Bella's betrothal, and him and King Theias thought it a good idea for the two to get to know one another. Prince Adonis made frequent visits, when he was not studying under his father. On those occasions, Ophion always was a constant companion for Adonis. I never knew why, but Ophion seemed to want this union more than anyone else," and Louis pondered on the idea for a moment before turning his attention back towards the couple. "I'm still grateful that Mary was always at Bella's side, keeping an eye on the two. She never did trust him. Now I sort of understand why. There's something not to trust about him. Even in the days before Bella set sail, he came alone to make sure that nothing would break up the engagement."

Drake felt his hand start to move and looked back up at his wife, who was now shaking. "What's wrong?"

"That... that week," started Izzy, her voice quivering. "I'll never forget those few days. He kept a constant eye on me, like I was some prize stallion that he was adding to his stable to be shown off."

"Bella, I'm so sorry. I had no idea," began Louis. "I'm glad Arthur convinced Dad to persuade him to leave before you."

"I wish he was on your ship," stated Drake, and the royal siblings both looked over at him with wide eyes.

"Why would you wish my sister to be around him any longer?"

"Because he would not be here today."

Silence filled the room, as the first true act of revenge that Drake had uttered since becoming Captain of the Tesoro came to light. Drake the Dread was back for that moment, and Izzy did not like seeing it one bit. The maddening idea switched gears in her mind and took her from the nervous wreck that she was becoming over the awful memories and slowly bringing her back to herself. "Drake, how could you say that?"

"He doesn't deserve to be alive for what he's done to you!"

"He's still a person," started Izzy, and Drake turned his back on the pair, as his anger was still boiling. "No one deserved to die that day, and you know it. Besides, what if your ship hadn't happened upon us? Everyone's lives could have been spared."

Drake's anger began to melt, thinking over what his wife had just said. He had not wanted to continue being what he had been since he saw Izzy again that faithful day, but he knew he would not be able to stile that part of him. The next notion then struck him in the heart, and he could not keep it from coming out of his mouth. "But we wouldn't have seen each other again…" and Izzy looked up at him. "I wish I hadn't killed those people, especially Mary, but I wouldn't have traded these last three years for anything in the world."

"And I couldn't have imagined this life without you in it," and she pulled Drake into a hug.

Seeing the true love between his sister and brother-in-law, Louis could feel in his heart that he could not separate them, no matter the costs. "Simple acts can change time. Father knew that. He was willing to follow his heart and let you have happiness, Bella. I should do the same. He would want it that way."

"No. Last time was different. Father could invent a story due to the circumstances. They won't be so easily deceived this time, Louis," spoke Izzy, as she made her way to stand in between the two men that she loved.

"What if I fight Prince Adonis?" questioned Drake, in which he caught both of their attentions. "It is a personal battle now. I won't lose her without a fight."

"Drake, I won't let you. If you beat Adonis, that will just anger Exousia even more, and you both will be hunted down the rest of your lives," responded Louis.

"The man must have some kind of honor to strike up a personal accord; one that would overpower a kingly bargain made almost a decade ago."

"I will hear of no such thing. Dauphin Magie has endured war before, and we can do it again. I must do what is right for my family."

As the two men quarreled over what was to be done with this new ultimatum, Izzy made her way over to the window to look out at her beautiful kingdom. She had grown up on this peaceful island, and it only remained in peace because of royal treaties due to the accord that her father and family before him had made with neighboring kingdoms. How could she let any harm come to those that worked so hard to make this kingdom a paradise to all those that lived here? It was time to put the sailor's hat away and replace the tiara on her head to be, who she was born to be. “I will go,” she quietly spoke, but the boys did not pause in their quarreling. “There’s no need to argue anymore. I have made my decision. I am going to Exousia.”

Those words ended the verbal feud, as Drake and Louis both turned their attention towards Izzy, now standing with the demeanor of a princess. “No, I won’t let you. There has to be another way!” spoke up Drake.

“No, there is not. Exousia is strict on accords. If I don’t go, they will burn our beautiful kingdom to the ground, and I could not live with myself knowing I would be the death of thousands of people,” and she turned to her brother, to avoid any more eye contact from her husband, knowing he would be the only one to change her mind. “Louis, you know deep down in your heart that this is the only thing to keep our kingdom safe. We were born and raised to protect our people, no matter the costs. You would do the same, if you were in my place.”

Not able to protest her words of truth, Louis closed his eyes and nodded his head. A moment later, he then wrapped his arms around his courageous sister and pulled her into a hug before whispering in her ear. “I wish I were in your place, Bella, so that you would not have to do this.”

Hearing her brother say that brought tears to her eyes but no words to her lips. She let it last a moment longer before turning back to her husband. “I’m so sorry, Drake.”

Seeing the honesty in her eyes, Drake had to try to mask the tears that appeared on his face. “There’s nothing I can do to change your mind?”

“I’ve already cost enough people their lives. I can’t be responsible for thousands more if I say no.”

Drake then reached out, took Izzy from her brother, and held her close to him, as Louis started to back away towards the door. The young king felt pain and guilt in his heart, as he knew he was selling his sister's happiness for a chance at peace. All he could do now was let them have one last night together, so he slipped out the door to inform Arthur to ready the royal ship for Princess Isabella's journey to Exousia.

Chapter Eleven

Polemos

Clouds filled the muggy morning, as the sun tried to break through. The royal family made their way down the marina, stopping just short of the docks under the protection of the stone archways. Izzy was starting to lose her royal composure now being so close to the Exousian ship. She thought she could return to her noble ways and do what needed to be done to ensure the safety of her people, but now the thought of being the person she no longer was absolutely terrified her. "Mom…" her voice quivered, as she reached for Elizabeth's hand and gripped it tightly. "Mom… can we talk please?"

"Of course, my dear," gently spoke the former queen, and she quietly pulled her daughter aside. "What is wrong?"

"When you married Daddy… did you do it out of love or because you had to for your kingdom?"

Elizabeth looked down for a moment, thinking on how to phrase her thoughts before speaking. In truth, she had married Philip through an arranged marriage similar to the fate of her daughter. Princesses were supposed to be married off as a peace treaty between kingdoms. It was a rarity that these royal women were able to marry someone outside of an arrangement, let alone someone from a different class. Being a princess was indeed a full-time job with responsibilities of devoting your entire life to your kingdom, no matter the cost. However, Philip was a very loving and devoted person from the instant she had met him.

"I was very lucky," began the regal woman. "Even though it was an arranged marriage and I had to leave my home and family, your father was someone I knew I was going to love from the moment I met him. He was never anything less than loyal and loving. And even though it may not be apparent right now, Prince Adonis is a gentleman. He has always been kind to you and nothing less than how a prince should treat a princess since the moment you met him."

"If he truly is this wonderful person, then why is he forcing us to marry? Hasn't he found someone else by now?" questioned the princess, her emotions coming more to light.

"Bella… I don't think this is Prince Adonis' doing," she spoke with an attempt at comforting words. "And when betrothals end, for whatever reason, it is always up to the kingdom to decide the fate of the person whose hand was a part of the arrangement. I do not know what King Theias or even Ophion have done and why Prince Adonis is still un-attached, but we do not need to worry about what could have been done. Always focus on the here and now. The past can never be changed, but the future can."

"Do you think I can be as happy as you were with Daddy?"

The former queen thought long and hard on her response. She knew deep down that Drake made her daughter happier than anyone else could ever make her. However, she did not want to send the princess off with no hope in her heart. It would set her up with nothing but a lifetime of misery. Elizabeth could not bear to inflict so much pain on

Izzy. "I think once you truly find peace with yourself and open your heart to let your new family in, will you find happiness," she finally spoke with a gentle smile.

Izzy wrapped her arms around her mother and held on to her tightly, as she whispered, "Thank you, Mommy."

All Elizabeth could do was hold her daughter close and hope that her words would ring true. She did not let go, as she did not know if she would ever see Izzy ever again, so she was going to make every moment count. Elizabeth then kissed the top of her daughter's head before moving down to kiss her brow and finally each of Izzy's cheeks. "You will be an amazing queen. Just remember to always rule from your heart."

"I will, Mother."

Elizabeth then looked into Izzy's eyes and tried to take a mental picture, so she would always remember her last private moment with her daughter. She wished that she would not have to send her daughter off, but it was Izzy's decision. Maybe one day she would be lucky enough to see her again. "You have my love to guide you on your journey."

Before the princess could speak up, she felt a tap on her shoulder and turned to see her brother behind her. She quickly wiped her eyes before the tears could fall and then flung her arms around Louis. "I'm sorry I put you in the middle of this difficult decision, Louis."

"I'm just sorry you have to leave Drake."

"It…" began Izzy and her voice caught in her throat. "It's… the right thing to do for our kingdom."

"Before you step on that ship, I have one last thing to show you," and he led his sister around a corner into a dark alley way. "She's here," whispered Louis, and a dark figure emerged.

"Drake..." softly spoke Izzy, as she ran over to her husband and jumped into his arms.

"I'll distract everyone for a few minutes," spoke Louis, and before either one of the sailors could thank him, he disappeared.

Izzy stared at her husband in disbelief. "I didn't think I was ever going to see you again."

"I couldn't let that happen. That's why I asked your brother to do this for us."

She then rested her head on his shoulder and began to cry into it. "Why is this happening to us?"

The sailor just kept his arms around his wife and tried to comfort her. "I don't know, but we only have a few minutes together. Let's not think on that."

"I can't help it. Soon I'll be boarding a ship, and I'll never see you again."

"I promise I will stay with you. No matter what," softly spoke Drake, not wanting to let her go.

Izzy leaned her head up and looked into Drake's eyes, knowing something was going on in his mind. "No, you can't come with me. They can't know that we're married."

"Till death do us part," whispered the sailor.

"Please don't say that," and tears started to fall down the princess' cheeks.

"Bella, we need to go," spoke up Louis, as he stepped back around the corner.

"I love you, Drake."

"I love you too, Izzy, and no matter what happens, I'll always be with you," whispered Drake and he kissed her goodbye before releasing her from his arms.

No other words could be found, as Louis took his sister's hand and gently escorted her away from her husband and back to their mother and the small group of palace guards. Everyone's heart was broken at the forced arrangement that was to be upheld, but they kept their regal faces on as they continued onward to the ship, Polemos, where Ophion was waiting for them. "Your excellency," bowed the royal visor.

"Ophion, this is your last chance to do the right thing. Let Princess Isabella out of this accord," pleaded King Louis, one last time on behalf of his sister.

"I am deeply sorry, King Louis, but we must always follow up on our agreements, unless you are suggesting that Dauphin Magie will never keep its end of the bargain. I would hate to see how many alliances would fall apart and your kingdom left without any support," spoke Ophion with a grin on his lips.

"Enough!" Izzy commanded, raising her voice. "My brother always honors agreements, as our father did before him. Now, there will be no more talk of this accord, as it is being honored," and Isabella turned to say goodbye to her family.

Before she could even get one last hug from her brother, the advisor of Exousia put his hand on the princess' shoulder and started to direct her in the direction of the gangplank. "I am deeply sorry, your highness, but we must set sail now in order to have you meeting with your future king by nightfall," spoke Ophion, and he started to pull the princess on board.

"Bella!" called out Louis, wanting to run after his sister, but was held back by his own guards.

"Louis! Mom! I love you both!" shouted Izzy, as she rushed to the edge and the gangplank was pulled in for the ship to sail away. The last image she saw of her remaining family was her mother crying and her brother holding on to their mother, as he watched her sail into the fog.

∞ ∞ ∞

Hours passed by, as Izzy sat on a crate near the railing of the ship. She clutched her journal that Mary had given her on her eleventh birthday and skimmed the pages to read all of the adventures that she had written down. Some were ones that she had read to Drake and others were ones that she experienced with him. Izzy wanted to pull out a quill and start writing in it again, but she could not find in her heart to do so. The pain was still too near.

"Sir!" called out the gentleman at the helm to Ophion. "There's a ship following us!" and Isabella jumped up from where she was at to look over the railing to spy a small merchant ship.

Ophion walked up past the helm and straight to the stern to get a look at it. "Send it down to the depths," he commanded.

Izzy's eyes grew wide, as she heard the command. "Wait!" she yelled, as she ran over towards her new advisor. "That's a merchant ship. There are innocent people on board. You can't do that to them."

"That ship has been following us ever since we left Dauphin Magie. It is clearly up to something and must be stopped."

The princess looked back at the ship once more and recognized it as the ship she spent her last few years on. Tears were beginning to form, thinking on what Drake had said to her right before they parted ways. “Please, I beg of you. Please spare the ship.”

“Ready the cannons!” called out Ophion, and the cannons were moved out on the Starboard side, as the ship made a slow turn to get proper aim.

“You can’t do this!”

“Aim!”

“NO!”

“FIRE!” and the cannons all sent out blasts.

Izzy rushed to the railing to see the cannonballs strike the small vessel. Within moments, fire and smoke filled the spot where the ship had been. She fell to her knees at the sight and could not hold back the sobs that filled her with grief beyond anything that she could comprehend. If her world was not crumbling down before, it was completely gone with that explosion.

It was in her anguish, which blocked out the very reality around her, that she did not notice the snake in the grass had taken a knee next to her. He moved a strand of hair away from her ear and whispered, “I knew about your marriage, and I knew he was going to come to try to save you. Well, it is hard to save a person when you’re dead.”

The princess turned her head to look at the disgusting man next to her. Words could not be formed to reveal how much anger, how much sorrow, how much hate she had in her very soul. All she could do was stare at him, as he stood up and walked away with a small laughter that lingered with her, long after he was out of sight.

It was only after the faint traces of black smoke that could no longer be seen amidst the fog that she made her self stand up. Her legs could barely keep her on her feet, as she felt nauseous and wanted nothing more than to hide away from the world. Slowly, Izzy made her way down to her private compartment and let herself fall on to her bed. Tears were still pouring from her eyes, as she pulled out her journal and let it fall beside her out of her hands. When she heard the small thud, she looked over to see something peeking out of the pages, so she picked up the book. What had fallen out was a red orchid that she had saved from her time in Valiaguila on her anniversary. She gently picked up the flower and mourned over her losses, now dreading more and more of what she will find when Polemos docks in Exousia.

Epilogue

To Carry Out an Accord

"Do you Adonis, Prince of Exousia, take Isabella, Princess of Dauphin Magie, to be your lady and princess?" asked the royal high priest of Exousia, as he stood before the Royal Court, nobility, and the bride and groom on the sand stone stage of the entrance to the palace.

"I do," replied the handsome prince, dressed in his finest attire with all of his medals of honor on show for the Court.

With a smile and a nod, the elder vicar turned his attention to the young girl, who was visibly shaking. "Do you, Isabella, Princess of Dauphin Magie, take Adonis, Prince of Exousia, to be your lord and prince?"

Izzy's mouth slightly opened, as she had difficulty making any sound come out. Slowly, her eyes looked around for any help. King Theias sat proudly nearby, watching the heir to his throne finish a peace treaty. No other face was recognized in her field of vision. No Mary to help her this time. Her soul was shattered. There was nothing left for her, now that she was separated from her family and the man that she loved.

As the silence ensued, a tall shadow slinked up behind her and whispered in her ear, “I would agree, if I were you, princess, or your happy little kingdom will cease to exist.”

The princess looked over shoulder at the snake, who’s voice echoed in her mind. *“It is hard to save a person when you’re dead.”* She was truly alone now, and she was the only person who could save her beloved Dauphin Magie from massacre.

As a tear sprang to her eye, she whispered. “I do.” It was only then that she felt the crown made out of ruby be placed on her head by Ophion.

“Your highness. My Lords and Ladies. People of the Kingdom of Exousia. It is now with great honor that I present to you, Adonis and Isabella, Prince and Princess of Exousia!” announced the priest, as he stepped back.

The newly wed royal couple then turned to face all of the cheering people of Exousia, and as Adonis waved to all of his royal subjects, Izzy just stood there with a single tear falling down her cheek. She was now to be trapped in this world forever, with no hope of escape, but it was what she was born and raised to do. To be a peace treaty. Her life was meant to have the glitz and glamor, but it was also there to ensure the safety of her people, no matter the costs. So, all she could do now was keep her dignitary face on for the show that was being put on around her.

∞ ∞ ∞

As the cheers rang on, without a hint of dying down, a person cloaked in black watched on with the masses far from the stage. He looked at the ground and shook his head at the faux enthusiasm that resonated on. “Do not worry, your highness, for hope is on the way,” he whispered to himself before turning towards the docks and disappearing from the view all together.

J.R. Baler

J.R. Baler was born in Georgia, but found her heart resided with magic. So, she relocated to central Florida, where she found not only magic but humanity. Her eyes were opened at seeing all of the different cultures and types of people bonded by multiple things. In seeing this, she found she wanted to do more good than before and spread love not hate. She took up writing to help spread the love and to remind people not to judge others based on what they have heard. Every person is unique and deserves a chance to show that they too have good inside them. J.R. wants to dedicate this book all those we have lost and loved. They have never truly left us.

Made in the USA
Middletown, DE
10 April 2019